THE K-FACTOR

THE K-FACTOR

by Harry Harrison

"We're losing a planet, Neel. I'm afraid that I can't ... understand it."

The bald and wrinkled head wobbled a bit on the thin neck, and his eyes were moist. Abravanel was a very old man. Looking at him, Neel realized for the first time just how old and close to death he was. It was a profoundly shocking thought.

"Pardon me, sir," Neel broke in, "but is it possible? To lose a planet, I mean. If the readings are done correctly, and the k-factor equations worked to the tenth decimal place, then it's really just a matter of adjustment, making the indicated corrections. After all, Societics is an exact science—"

"Exact? *Exact!* Of course it's not! Have I taught you so little that you dare say that to me?" Anger animated the old man, driving the shadow of death back a step or two.

Neel hesitated, feeling his hands quiver ever so slightly, groping for the right words. Societics was his faith, and his teacher, Abravanel, its only prophet. This man before him, carefully preserved by the age-retarding drugs, was unique in the galaxy. A living anachronism, a refugee from the history books. Abravanel had singlehandedly worked out the equations, spelled out his science of Societics. Then he had trained seven generations of students in its fundamentals. Hearing the article of his faith defamed by its creator produced a negative feedback loop in Neel so strong his hands vibrated in tune with it. It took a jarring effort to crack out of the cycle.

"The laws that control Societics, as postulated by ... you, are as exact as any others in the unified-field theory universe."

"No they're not. And, if any man I taught believes that nonsense, I'm retiring tomorrow and dropping dead the day after. My science—and it is really not logical to call it a science—is based on observation, experimentation, control groups and corrected observations. And though we have made observations in the millions, we are dealing in units in the billions, and the interactions of these units are multiples of that. And let us never forget that our units are people who, when they operate as individuals, do so in a completely different manner. So you cannot truthfully call my theories exact. They fit the facts well enough and produce results in practice, that has been empirically proven. So far. Some day, I am sure, we will run across a culture that doesn't fit my rules. At that time the rules will have to be revised. We may have that situation now on Himmel. There's trouble cooking there."

"They have always had a high activity count, sir," Neel put in hopefully.

"High yes, but *always* negative. Until now. Now it is slightly positive and nothing we can do seems to change it. That's why I've called you in. I want you to run a new basic survey, ignoring the old one still in operation, to re-examine the check points on our graphs. The trouble may lie there."

Neel thought before he answered, picking his words carefully. "Wouldn't that be a little ... unethical, sir? After all Hengly, who is operator there now, is a friend of mine. Going behind his back, you know."

"I know nothing of the sort." Abravanel snorted. "We are not playing for poker chips, or seeing who can get a paper published first. Have you forgotten what Societics is?"

Neel answered by rote. "The applied study of the interaction of individuals in a culture, the interaction of the group generated by these individuals, the equations derived therefrom, and the application of these equations to control one or more factors of this same culture."

"And what is the one factor that we have tried to control in order to make all the other factors possible of existence?"

"War." Neel said, in a very small voice.

"Very good then, there is no doubt what it is we are talking about. You are going to land quietly on Himmel, do a survey as quickly as possible and transmit the data back here. There is no cause to think of it as sneaking behind Hengly's back, but as doing something to help him set the matter right. Is that understood?"

"Yes, sir," Neel said firmly this time, straightening his back and letting his right hand rest reassuringly on the computer slung from his belt.

"Excellent. Then it is now time to meet your assistant." Abravanel touched a button on his desk.

*

It was an unexpected development and Neel waited with interest as the door opened. But he turned away abruptly, his eyes slitted and his face white with anger. Abravanel introduced them.

"Neel Sidorak, this is—"

"Costa. I know him. He was in my class for six months." There wasn't the slightest touch of friendliness in Neel's voice now. Abravanel either ignored it or didn't hear it. He went on as if the two cold, distant young men were the best of friends.

"Classmates. Very good—then there is no need to make introductions. Though it might be best to make clear your separate areas of control. This is your project Neel, and Adao Costa will be your assistant, following your orders and doing whatever he can to help. You know he isn't a graduate Societist, but he has done a lot of field work for us and can help you greatly in that. And, of course, he will be acting as an observer for the UN, and making his own reports in this connection."

Neel's anger was hot and apparent. "So he's a UN observer now. I wonder if he still holds his old job at the same time. I think it only fair, sir, that you know. He works for Interpol."

Abravanel's ancient and weary eyes looked at both men, and he sighed. "Wait outside Costa," he said, "Neel will be with you in a minute."

Costa left without a word and Abravanel waved Neel back to his chair. "Listen to me now," he said, "and stop playing tunes on that infernal buzzer." Neel snapped his hand away from the belt computer, as if it had suddenly grown hot. A hesitant finger reached out to clear the figures he had nervously been setting up, then thought better of it. Abravanel sucked life into his ancient pipe and squinted at the younger man.

"Listen," he said. "You have led a very sheltered life here at the university, and that is probably my fault. No, don't look angry, I don't mean about girls. In that matter undergraduates have been the same for centuries. I'm talking about people in groups, individuals, politics, and all the complicated mess that makes up human life. This has been your area of study and the program is carefully planned so you can study it secondhand. The important thing is to develop the abstract viewpoint, since any attempt to prejudge results can only mean disaster. And it has been proved many times that a man with a certain interest will make many unwitting errors to shape an observation or experiment in favor of his interest. No, we could have none of that here.

"We are following the proper study of mankind and we must do that by keeping personally on the outside, to preserve our perspective. When you understand that, you understand many small things about the university. Why we give only resident student scholarships at a young age, and why the out-of-the-way location here in the Dolomites. You will also see the reason why the campus bookstore stocks all of the books published, but never has an adequate supply of newspapers. The agreed policy has been to see that you all mature with the long view. Then—hopefully—you will be immune to short-term political interests after you leave.

"This policy has worked well in turning out men with the correct attitude towards their work. It has also turned out a fair number of self-centered, egocentric horrors."

*

Neel flushed. "Do you mean that I—"

"No, I don't mean you. If I did, I would say so. Your worst fault—if you can call it a fault, since it is the very thing we have been trying to bring about—is that you have a very provincial attitude towards the universe. Now is the time to re-examine some of those ideas. Firstly, what do you think the attitude of the UN is towards Societics?"

There was no easy answer, Neel could see traps ready for anything he said. His words were hesitant. "I can't say I've really ever thought about it. I imagine the UN would be in favor of it, since we make their job of world government that much easier—"

"No such thing," Abravanel said, tempering the sharpness of his words with a smile. "To put it in the simplest language, they hate our guts. They wish I had never formulated Societics, and at the same time they are very glad I did. They are in the position of the man who caught the tiger by the tail. The man enjoys watching the tiger eat all of his enemies, but as each one is consumed his worry grows greater. What will happen when the last one is gone? Will the tiger then turn and eat him?

"Well—we are the UN's tiger. Societics came along just at the time it was sorely needed. Earth had settled a number of planets, and governed them. First as outposts, then as colonies. The most advanced planets very quickly outgrew the colony stage and flexed their independent muscles. The UN had no particular desire to rule an empire, but at the same time they had to insure Earth's safety. I imagine they were considering all sorts of schemes—including outright military control—when they came to me.

"Even in its early, crude form, Societics provided a stopgap that would give them some breathing time. They saw to it that my work was well endowed and aided me—unofficially of course—in setting up the first control experiments on different planets. We had results, some very good, and the others not so bad that the local police couldn't get things back under control after a while. I was, of course, happy to perfect my theories in practice. After a hundred years I had all the rough spots evened down and we were in business. The UN has never come up with a workable alternative plan, so they have settled down to the uncomfortable business of holding the tiger's tail. They worry and spend vast sums of money keeping an eye on our work."

"But *why?*" Neel broke in.

"Why?" Abravanel gave a quick smile. "Thank you for fine character rating. I imagine it is inconceivable to you that I might want to be Emperor of the Universe. I could be, you know. The same forces that hold the lids on the planets could just as easily blow them off."

Neel was speechless at the awful enormity of the thought. Abravanel rose from behind his desk with an effort, and shambled over to lay a thin and feather-light arm on the younger man's shoulders. "Those are the facts of life my boy. And since we cannot escape them, we must live with them. Costa is just a man doing his duty. So try and put up with him. For my sake if not for your own."

"Of course," Neel agreed quickly. "The whole thing takes a bit of getting used to, but I think I can manage. We'll do as good a job on Himmel as it is possible to do. Don't worry about me, sir."

*

Costa was waiting in the next room, puffing quietly on a long cigarette. They left together, walking down the hall in silence. Neel glanced sideways at the wiry, dark-skinned Brazilian and wondered what he could say to smooth things out. He still had his reservations about Costa, but he'd keep them to himself now. Abravanel had ordered peace between them, and what the old man said was the law.

It was Costa who spoke first. "Can you brief me on Himmel—what we'll find there, and be expected to do?"

"Run the basic survey first, of course," Neel told him. "Chances are that that will be enough to straighten things out. Since the completion last year of the refining equations of Debir's Postulate, all sigma-110 and alpha-142 graph points are suspect—"

"Just stop there please, and run the flag back down the pole." Costa interrupted. "I had a six-months survey of Societics seven years ago, to give me a general idea of the field. I've worked with survey teams since then, but I have only the vaguest idea of the application of the information we got. Could you cover the ground again—only a bit slower?"

Neel controlled his anger successfully and started again, in his best classroom manner.

"Well, I'm sure you realize that a good survey is half the problem. It must be impartial and exact. If it is accurately done, application of the k-factor equations is almost mechanical."

"You've lost me again. Everyone always talks about the k-factor, but no one has ever explained just what it is."

Neel was warming to his topic now. "It's a term borrowed from nucleonics, and best understood in that context. Look, you know how an atomic pile works—essentially just like an atomic bomb. The difference is just a matter of degree and control. In both of them you have neutrons tearing around, some of them hitting nuclei and starting new neutrons going. These in turn hit and start others. This goes on faster and faster and *bam*, a few milliseconds later you have an atomic bomb. This is what happens if you don't attempt to control the reaction.

"However, if you have something like heavy water or graphite that will slow down neutrons and an absorber like cadmium, you can alter the speed of the reaction. Too much damping material will absorb too many neutrons and the reaction will stop. Not enough and the reaction will build up to an explosion. Neither of these extremes is wanted in an atomic pile. What is needed is a happy balance where you are soaking up just as many neutrons as are being generated all the time. This will give you a constant temperature inside the reactor. The net neutron reproduction constant is then 1. This balance of neutron generation and absorption is the k-factor of the reactor. Ideally 1.0000000.

"That's the ideal, though, the impossible to attain in a dynamic system like a reactor. All you need is a few more neutrons around, giving you a k-factor of 1.00000001 and you are headed for trouble. Each extra neutron produces two and your production rate soars geometrically towards bang. On the other hand, a k-factor of 0.999999999 is just as bad. Your reaction is spiraling down in the other direction. To control a pile you watch your k-factor and make constant adjustments."

"All this I follow," Costa said, "but where's the connection with Societics?"

"We'll get to that—just as soon as you realize and admit that a minute difference of degree can produce a marked difference of kind. You might say that a single, impossibly tiny, neutron is the difference between an atom bomb and a slowly cooling pile of inert uranium isotopes. Does that make sense?"

"I'm staggering, but still with you."

"Good. Then try to go along with the analogy that a human society is like an atomic pile. At one extreme you will have a dying, decadent culture—the remains of a highly mechanized society—living off its capital, using up resources it can't replace because of a lost technology. When the last machine breaks and the final food synthesizer collapses the people will die. This is the cooled down atomic pile. At the other extreme is complete and violent anarchy. Every man thinking only of himself, killing and destroying anything that gets in his way—the atomic explosion. Midway between the two is a vital, active, producing society.

"This is a generalization—and you must look at it that way. In reality society is infinitely complex, and the ramifications and possibilities are endless. It can do a lot more things than fizzle or go boom. Pressure of population, war or persecution patterns can cause waves of immigration. Plant and animal species can be wiped out by momentary needs or fashions. Remember the fate of the passenger pigeon and the American bison.

"All the pressures, cross-relationships, hungers, needs, hatreds, desires of people are reflected in their interrelationships. One man standing by himself tells us nothing. But as soon as he says something, passes on information in an altered form, or merely expresses an attitude—he becomes a reference point. He can be marked, measured and entered on a graph. His actions can be grouped with others and the action of the group measured. Man—and his society—then becomes a systems problem that can be fed into a computer. We've cut the Gordian knot of the three-L's and are on our way towards a solution."

*

"Stop!" Costa said, raising his hand. "I was with you as far as the 3L's. What are they? A private code?"

"Not a code—abbreviation. Linear Logic Language, the pitfall of all the old researchers. All of them, historians, sociologists, political analysts, anthropologists, were licked before they started. They had to know all about A and B before they could find C. Facts to them were always hooked up in a series. Whereas in truth they had to be analyzed as a complex circuit complete with elements like positive and negative feedback, and crossover switching. With the whole thing being stirred up constantly by continual homeostasis correction. It's little wonder they did do badly."

"You can't really say that," Adao Costa protested. "I'll admit that Societics has carried the art tremendously far ahead. But there were many basics that had already been discovered."

"If you are postulating a linear progression from the old social sciences—forget it," Neel said. "There is the same relationship here that alchemy holds to physics. The old boys with their frog guts and awful offal knew a bit about things like distilling and smelting. But there was no real order to their knowledge, and it was all an unconsidered by-product of their single goal, the whole nonsense of transmutation."

They passed a lounge, and Adao waved Neel in after him, dropping into a chair. He rummaged through his pockets for a cigarette, organizing his thoughts. "I'm still with you," he said. "But how do we work this back to the k-factor?"

"Simple," Neel told him. "Once you've gotten rid of the 3L's and their false conclusions. Remember that politics in the old days was all We are angels and They are devils. This was literally believed. In the history of mankind there has yet to be a war that wasn't backed by the official clergy on each side. And each declared that God was on their side. Which leaves You Know Who as prime supporter of the enemy. This theory is no more valid than the one that a single man can lead a country into war, followed by the inference that a well-timed assassination can save the peace."

"That doesn't sound too unreasonable," Costa said.

"Of course not. All of the old ideas sound good. They have a simple-minded simplicity that anyone can understand. That doesn't make them true. Kill a war-minded dictator and nothing changes. The violence-orientated society, the factors that produced it, the military party that represents it—none of these are changed. The k-factor remains the same."

"There's that word again. Do I get a definition yet?"

Neel smiled. "Of course. The k-factor is one of the many factors that interrelate in a society. Abstractly it is no more important than the other odd thousand we work with. But in practice it is the only one we try to alter."

"The k-factor is the war factor," Adao Costa said. All the humor was gone now.

"That's a good enough name for it," Neel said, grinding out his half-smoked cigarette. "If a society has a positive k-factor, even a slight one that stays positive, then you are going to have a war. Our planetary operators have two jobs. First to gather and interpret data. Secondly to keep the k-factor negative."

They were both on their feet now, moved by the same emotion.

"And Himmel has a positive one that stays positive," Costa said. Neel Sidorak nodded agreement. "Then let's get into the ship and get going," he said.

*

It was a fast trip and a faster landing. The UN cruiser cut its engines and dropped like a rock in free fall. Night rain washed the ports and the computer cut in the maximum permissible blast for the minimum time that would reduce their speed to zero at zero altitude. Deceleration sat on their chests and squeezed their bones to rubber. Something crunched heavily under their stern at the exact instant the drive cut out. Costa was unbelted and out the door while Neel was still feeling his insides shiver back into shape.

The unloading had an organized rhythm that rejected Neel. He finally realized he could help best by standing back out of the way while the crewmen grav-lifted the heavy cases out through the cargo port, into the blackness of the rain-lashed woods. Adao Costa supervised this and seemed to know what he was doing. A signal rating wearing earphones stood to one side of the lock chanting numbers that sounded like detector fixes. There was apparently enough time to unload everything—but none to spare. Things got close towards the end.

Neel was suddenly bustled out into the rain and the last two crates were literally thrown out after him. He plowed through the mud to the edge of the clearing and had just enough time to cover his face before the take-off blast burst out like a new sun.

"Sit down and relax," Costa told him. "Everything is in the green so far. The ship wasn't spotted on the way down. Now all we have to do is wait for transportation."

In theory at least, Adao Costa was Neel's assistant. In practice he took complete charge of moving their equipment and getting it under cover in the capital city of Kitezh. Men and trucks appeared to help them, and vanished as soon as their work was done. Within twenty hours they were installed in a large loft, all of the machines uncrated and plugged in. Neel took a no-sleep and began tuning checks on all the circuits, glad of something to do. Costa locked the heavy door behind their last silent helper, then dropped gratefully onto one of the bedding rolls.

"How did the gadgets hold up?" he asked.

"I'm finding out now. They're built to take punishment—but being dropped twelve feet into mud soup, then getting baked by rockets isn't in the original specs."

"They crate things well these days," Costa said unworriedly, sucking on a bottle of the famous Himmelian beer. "When do you go to work?"

"We're working right now," Neel told him, pulling a folder of papers out of the file. "Before we left I drew up a list of current magazines and newspapers I would need. You can start on these. I'll have a sampling program planned by the time you get back."

Costa groaned hollowly and reached for the papers.

*

Once the survey was in operation it went ahead of its own momentum. Both men grabbed what food and sleep they could. The computers gulped down Neel's figures and spat out tape-reels of answers that demanded even more facts. Costa and his unseen helpers were kept busy supplying the material.

Only one thing broke the ordered labors of the week. Neel blinked twice at Costa before his equation-fogged brain assimilated an immediate and personal factor.

"You've a bandage on your head," he said. "A *blood-stained* bandage!"

"A little trouble in the streets. Mobs. And that's an incredible feat of observation," Costa marveled. "I had the feeling that if I came in here stark naked, you wouldn't notice it."

"I ... I get involved," Neel said. Dropping the papers on a table and kneading the tired furrow between his eyes. "Get wrapped up in the computation. Sorry. I tend to forget about people."

"Don't feel sorry to me," Costa said. "You're right. Doing the job. I'm supposed to help you, not pose for the *before* picture in Home Hospital ads. Anyway—how are we doing? Is there going to be a war? Certainly seems like one brewing outside. I've seen two people lynched who were only suspected of being Earthies."

"Looks don't mean a thing," Neel said, opening two beers. "Remember the analogy of the pile. It boils liquid metal and cooks out energy from the infrared right through to hard radiation. Yet it keeps on generating power at a nice, steady rate. But your A-bomb at zero minus one second looks as harmless as a fallen log. It's the k-factor that counts, not surface appearance. This planet may look like a dictator's dream of glory, but as long as we're reading in the negative things are fine."

"And how are things? How's our little k-factor?"

"Coming out soon," Neel said, pointing at the humming computer. "Can't tell about it yet. You never can until the computation is complete. There's a temptation to try and guess from the first figures, but they're meaningless. Like trying to predict the winner of a horse race by looking at the starters lined up at the gate."

"Lots of people think they can."

"Let them. There are few enough pleasures in this life without taking away all delusions."

Behind them the computer thunked and was suddenly still.

"This is it," Neel said, and pulled out the tape. He ran it quickly through his fingers, mumbling under his breath. Just once he stopped and set some figures into his hand computer. The result flashed in the window and he stared at it, unmoving.

"Good? Bad? What is it?"

Neel raised his head and his eyes were ten years older.

"Positive. Bad. Much worse than it was when we left Earth."

"How much time do we have?"

"Don't know for certain," Neel shrugged. "I can set it up and get an approximation. But there is no definite point on the scale where war *has* to break out. Just a going and going until, somewhere along the line—"

"I know. Gone." Costa said, reaching for his gun. He slid it into his side pocket. "Now it's time to stop looking and start doing. What do I do?"

"Going to kill War Marshal Lommeord?" Neel asked distastefully. "I thought we had settled that you can't stop a war by assassinating the top man."

"We also settled that *something* can be done to change the k-factor. The gun is for my own protection. While you're radioing results back to Earth and they're feeling bad about it, I'm going to be doing something. Now *you* tell me what that something is."

This was a different man from the relaxed and quietly efficient Adao Costa of the past week. All of his muscles were hard with the restrained energy of an animal crouching to leap. The gun, ready in his pocket, had a suddenly new significance. Neel looked away, reaching around for words. This was all very alien to him and suddenly a little frightening. It was one thing to work out a k-problem in class, and discuss the theory of correction.

It was something entirely different to direct the operation.

"Well?" Costa's voice knifed through his thoughts.

"You can ... well ... it's possible to change one of the peak population curves. Isolate individuals and groups, then effect status and location changes—"

"You mean get a lot of guys to take jobs in other towns through the commercial agents?"

Neel nodded.

"Too slow." Costa withered the idea with his voice. "Fine in the long run, but of absolutely no value in an emergency." He began to pace back and forth. Too quickly. It was more of a bubbling-over than a relaxation. "Can't you isolate some recent key events that can be reversed?"

"It's possible." Neel thought about it, quickly. "It wouldn't be a final answer, just a delaying action."

"That's good enough. Tell me what to do."

Neel flipped through his books of notes, checking off the Beta-13's. These were the reinforcers, the individuals and groups who were k-factor amplifiers. It was a long list which he cut down quickly by crossing off the low increment additions and multiple groups. Even while the list was incomplete, Neel began to notice a pattern. It was an unlikely one, but it was there. He isolated the motivator and did a frequency check. Then sat back and whistled softly.

"We have a powerhouse here," he said, flipping the paper across the table. "Take this organization out of the equations and you might even knock us negative."

"Society for the Protection of the Native Born," Costa read. "Doesn't sound like very important. Who or what are they?"

"Proof positive of the law of averages. It's possible to be dealt a royal flush in a hand of cards, but it isn't very common. It's just as possible for a bunch of simpletons to set up an organization for one purpose, and have it turn out to be a supercharged, high-frequency k-factor amplifier. That's what's happened with this infernal S.P.N.B. A seedy little social club, dedicated to jingoists with low I.Q.'s. With the war scare they have managed to get hold of a few credits. They have probably been telling the same inflated stories for years about the discrimination against natives of this fair planet, but no one has really cared. Now they have a chance to get their news releases and faked pix out in quantity. Just at a time when the public is ripe for their brand of nonsense. Putting this bunch out of business will be a good day's work."

"Won't there be repercussions?" Costa asked. "If they are this important and throw so much weight around—won't it look suspicious if they are suddenly shut up. Like an obvious move by the enemy?"

"Not at all. That might be true if, for instance, you blew up the headquarters of the War Party. It would certainly be taken as an aggressive move. But no one really knows or cares about this Society of the Half-baked Native Born. There might be reaction and interest if attention was drawn to them. But if some accident or act of nature were to put them out of business, that would be the end of it."

Costa was snapping his lighter on and off as he listened to Neel, staring at the flame. He closed it and held it up. "I believe in accidents. I believe that even in our fireproof age, fires still occur. Buildings still burn down. And if a burnt building just happened to be occupied by the S.P.N.B.—just one tenant of many—and their offices and records were destroyed; that would be of very little interest to anyone except the fire brigade."

"You're a born criminal," Neel told him. "I'm glad we're on the same side. That's your department and I leave it to you. I'll just listen for the news flashes. Meanwhile I have one little errand to take care of."

The words stopped Costa, who was almost out the door. He turned stiffly to look at Neel putting papers into an envelope. Yet Costa spoke naturally, letting none of his feelings through into his voice.

"Where are you going?"

"To see Hengly, the planetary operator here. Abravanel told me to stay away from him, to run an entirely new basic survey. Well we've done that now, and pinpointed some of the trouble areas as well. I can stop feeling guilty about poaching another man's territory and let him know what's going on."

"No. Stay away from Hengly," Costa said. "The last thing in the world we want to do, is to be seen near him. There's a chance that he ... well ... might be compromised."

"What do you mean!" Neel snapped. "Hengly's a friend of mine, a graduate—"

"He might also be surrounded ten deep by the secret police. Did you stop to think about *that?*"

Neel hadn't thought about it, and his anger vanished when he did. Costa drove the point home.

"Societics has been a well kept secret for over two centuries. It may still be a secret—or bits of it might have leaked out. And even if the Himmelians know nothing about Societics, they have certainly heard of espionage. They know the UN has agents on their world, they might think Hengly is one of them. This is all speculation, of course, but we do have one fact—this Society of Native Boobs we turned up. *We* had no trouble finding them. If Hengly had reliable field men, he should know about them, too. The only reason he hasn't is because he isn't getting the information. Which means he's compromised."

Reaching back for a chair, Neel fell heavily into it. "You're right ... of course! I never realized."

"Good," Costa said. "We'll do something to help Hengly tomorrow, but this operation comes first. Sit tight. Get some rest. And don't open the door for anyone except me."

*

It had been a long job—and a tiring one—but it was almost over. Neel allowed himself the luxury of a long yawn, then shuffled over to the case of rations they had brought. He stripped the seal from something optimistically labeled CHICKEN DINNER—it tasted just like the algae it had been made from—and boiled some coffee while it was heating.

And all the time he was doing these prosaic tasks his mind was turning an indigestible fact over and over. It wasn't a conscious process, but it was nevertheless going on. The automatic mechanism of his brain ran it back and forth like a half heard tune, searching for its name. Neel was tired, or he would have reacted sooner. The idea finally penetrated. One fact he had taken for granted was an obvious impossibility.

The coffee splashed to the floor as he jumped to his feet.

"It's wrong ... it *has* to be wrong!" he said aloud, grabbing up the papers. Computations and graphs dropped and were trampled into the spilled coffee. When he finally found the one he wanted his hands were shaking as he flipped through it. The synopsis of Hengly's reports for the past five years. The gradual rise and fall of the k-factor from month to month. There were no sharp breaks in the curve or gaps in the supporting equations.

Societics isn't an exact science. But it's exact enough to know when it is working with incomplete or false information. If Hengly had been kept in the dark about the S.P.N.B., he would also have been misinformed about other factors. This kind of alteration of survey would *have* to show in the equations.

It didn't.

Time was running out and Neel had to act. But what to do? He must warn Adao Costa. And the records here had to be protected. Or better yet destroyed. There was a power in these machines and charts that couldn't be allowed to fall into nationalist hands. But what could be done about it?

In all the welter of equipment and containers, there was one solid, heavy box that he had never opened. It belonged to Costa, and the UN man had never unlocked it in his presence. Neel looked at the heavy clasps on it and felt defeat. But when he pulled at the lid, wondering what to do next, it fell open. It hadn't been sealed. Costa wasn't the kind of man who did things by accident. He had looked forward to the time when Neel might need what was in this box, and had it ready.

Inside was just what Neel expected. Grenades, guns, some smoothly polished devices that held an aura of violence. Looking at them, Neel had an overwhelming sensation of defeat. His life was dedicated to peace and the furthering of peace. He hated the violence that seemed inborn in man, and detested all the hypocritical rationalizations, such as the ends justifying the means. All of his training and personal inclinations were against it.

And he reached down and removed the blunt, black gun.

There was one other thing he recognized in the compact arsenal—a time bomb. There had been lectures on this mechanism in school, since the fact was clearly recognized that a time might come when equipment had to be destroyed rather than fall into the wrong hands. He had never seen one since, but he had learned the lesson well. Neel pushed the open chest nearer to his instruments and set the bomb dial for fifteen minutes. He slipped the gun into his pocket, started the fuse, and carefully locked the door when he left.

The bridges were burned. Now he had to find Adao Costa.

This entire operation was outside of his experience and knowledge. He could think of no plan that could possibly make things easier or safer. All he could do was head for the offices of the Society for the Protection of the Native Born and hope he could catch Adao before he ran into any trouble.

*

Two blocks away from the address he heard the sirens. Trying to act as natural as the other pedestrians, he turned to look as the armored cars and trucks hurtled by. Packed with armed police, their sirens and revolving lights cleared a path through the dark streets. Neel kept walking, following the cars now.

The street he wanted to go into was cordoned off.

Showing more than a normal interest would have been a giveaway. He let himself be hurried past, with no more than a glance down the block, with the other pedestrians. Cars and men were clustered around a doorway that Neel felt sure was number 265, his destination. Something was very wrong.

Had Costa walked into a trap—or tripped an alarm? It didn't really matter which, either way the balloon had gone up. Neel walked on slowly, painfully aware of his own inadequacy in dealing with the situation. It was a time for action—but what action? He hadn't the slightest idea where Costa was or how he could be of help to him.

Halfway down the block there was a dark mouth of an alleyway—unguarded. Without stopping to think, Neel turned into it. It would bring him closer to the building. Perhaps Costa was still trapped in there. He could get in, help him.

The back of 265 was quiet, with no hint of the activity on the other side of the building. Neel had counted carefully and was sure he had the right one. It was completely dark in the unlit alley, but he found a recessed door by touch. The chances were it was locked, but he moved into the alcove and leaned his weight against it, pulling at the handle, just in case. Nothing moved.

An inch behind his back the alley filled with light, washed with it, eye burning and strong. His eyes snapped shut, but he forced them open again, blinking against the pain. There were searchlights at each end of the alley, sealing it off. He couldn't get out.

In the instant before the fear hit him he saw the blood spots on the ground. There were three of them, large and glistening redly wet. They extended in a straight line away from him, pointing towards the gaping entrance of a cellar.

When the lights went out, Neel dived headlong towards the cracked and filthy pavement. The darkness meant that the police were moving slowly towards him from both ends of the alley, trapping him in between. There was nothing doubtful about the fate of an armed Earthman caught here. He didn't care. Neel's fear wasn't gone—he just had not time to think about it. His long shot had paid off and there was still a chance he could get Costa out of the trap he had let him walk into.

The lights had burned an after-image into his retina. Before it faded he reached out and felt his fingers slide across the dusty ground into a patch of wetness. He scrubbed at it with his sleeve, soaking up the blood, wiping the spot fiercely. With his other hand he pushed together a pile of dust and dirt, spreading it over the stain. As soon as he was sure the stain was covered he slid forward, groping for the second telltale splash.

Time was his enemy and he had no way to measure it. He could have been lying in the rubble of that alley for an hour—or a second. What was to be done, had to be done at once without a sound. There were silent, deadly men coming towards him through the darkness.

After the second smear was covered there was a drawn out moment of fear when he couldn't find the third and last. His fingers touched it finally, much farther on than he had expected. Time had certainly run out. Yet he forced himself to do as good a job here as he had with the other two. Only when it was dried and covered did he allow himself to slide forward into the cellar entrance.

Everything was going too fast. He had time for a single deep breath before the shriek of a whistle paralyzed him again. Footsteps slapped towards him and one of the searchlights burned with light. The footsteps speeded up and the man ran by, close enough for Neel to touch if he had reached out a hand. His clothing was shapeless and torn, his head and face thick with hair. That was all Neel had time to see before the guns roared and burned the life from the runner.

Some derelict, sleeping in the alley, who had paid with his life for being in the wrong spot at the wrong time. But his death had bought Neel a little more time. He turned and looked into the barrel of a gun.

Shock after shock had destroyed his capacity for fear. There was nothing left that could move him, even his own death. He looked quietly—dully—at the muzzle of the gun. With slow determination his mind turned over and he finally realized that this time there was nothing to fear.

"It's me, Adao," he whispered. "You'll be all right now."

"Ahh, it is you—" the voice came softly out of the darkness, the gun barrel wavered and sank. "Lift me up so I can get at this door. Can't seem to stand too well any more."

*

Neel reached down, found Costa's shoulders and slowly dragged him to his feet. His eyes were adjusting to the glare above them now, and he could make out the gleam of reflected light on the metal in Costa's fingers. The UN man's other hand was clutched tightly to his waist. The gun had vanished. The metal device wasn't a key, but Costa used it like one. It turned in the lock and the door swung open under their weight. Neel half carried, half dragged the other man's dead weight through it, dropping him to the floor inside. Before he closed the door he reached down and felt a great pool of blood outside.

There was no time to do a perfect job, the hard footsteps were coming, just a few yards away. His sleeves were sodden with blood as he blotted, then pushed rubble into the stain. He pulled back inside and the door closed with only the slightest click.

"I don't know how you managed it, but I'm glad you found me," Costa said. There was weakness as well as silence in his whisper.

"It was only chance I found you," Neel said bitterly. "But criminal stupidity on my part that let you walk into this trap."

"Don't worry about it, I knew what I was getting into. But I still had to go. Spring the trap to see if it *was* a trap."

"You suspected then that Hengly was—" Neel couldn't finish the sentence. He knew what he wanted to say, but the idea was too unbearable to put into words. Costa had no such compunction.

"Yes. Dear Hengly, graduate of the University and Practitioner of Societics. A traitor. A warmonger, worse than any of his predecessors because he knew just what to sell and how to sell it. It's never happened before ... but there was always the chance ... the weight of responsibility was too much ... he gave in—" Costa's voice had died away almost to a whisper. Then it was suddenly loud again, no louder than normal speaking volume, but sounding like a shout in the secret basement.

"Neel!"

"It's all right. Take it easy—"

"Nothing is all right—don't you realize that. I've been sending my reports back, so the UN and your Societics people will know how to straighten this mess out. But Hengly can turn this world upside down and might even get a shooting-war going before they get here. I'm out of it, but I can tell you who to contact, people who'll help. Hold the k-factor down—"

"That wouldn't do any good," Neel said quietly. "The whole thing is past the patch and polish stage now. Besides—I blew the whole works up. My machines and records, your—"

"You're a fool!" For the first time there was pain in Costa's voice.

"No. I was before—but not any more. As long as I thought it was a normal problem I was being outguessed at every turn. You must understand the ramifications of Societics. To a good operator there is no interrelationship that cannot be uncovered. Hengly would be certain to keep his eyes open for another field check. Our kind of operation is very easy to spot if you know where—and how—to look. The act of getting information implies contact of some kind, that contact can be detected. He's had our location marked and has been sitting tight, buying time. But our time ran out when you showed them we were ready to fight back. That's why I destroyed our setup, and cut our trail."

"But ... then we're defenseless! What can we possibly do?"

Neel knew the answer, but he hesitated to put it into words. It would be final then. He suddenly realized he had forgotten about Costa's wound.

"I'm sorry ... I forgot about your being hurt. What can I do?"

"Nothing," Costa snapped. "I put a field dressing on, that'll do. Answer my question. What is there left? What can be done now?"

"I'll have to kill Hengly. That will set things right until the team gets here."

"But what good will that accomplish?" Costa asked, trying to see the other man in the darkness of the cellar. "You told me yourself that a war couldn't be averted by assassination. No one individual means that much."

"Only in a normal situation," Neel explained. "You must look at the power struggle between planets as a kind of celestial chess game. It has its own rules. When I talked about individuals earlier I was talking about pieces on this chessboard. What I'm proposing now is a little more dramatic. I'm going to win the chess game in a slightly more unorthodox way. I'm going to shoot the other chess player."

There was silence for a long moment, broken only by the soft sigh of their breathing. Then Costa stirred and there was the sound of metal clinking slightly on the floor.

"It's really my job," Costa said, "but I'm no good for it. You're right, you'll have to go. But I can help you, plan it so you will be able to get to Hengly. You might even stand a better chance than me, because you are so obviously an amateur. Now listen carefully, because we haven't much time."

Neel didn't argue. He knew what needed doing, but Costa could tell him how best to go about it. The instructions were easy to memorize, and he put the weapons away as he was told.

"Once you're clear of this building, you'll have to get cleaned up," Costa said. "But that's the only thing you should stop for. Get to Hengly while he is still rattled, catch him off guard as much as possible. Then—after you finish with him—dig yourself in. Stay hidden at least three days before you try to make any contacts. Things should have quieted down a bit by then."

"I don't like leaving you here," Neel said.

"It's the best way, as well as being the only way. I'll be safe enough. I've a nice little puncture in me, but there's enough medication to see me through."

"If I'm going to hole up, I'll hole up here. I'll be back to take care of you."

Costa didn't answer him. There was nothing more to say. They shook hands in the darkness and Neel crawled away.

*

There was little difficulty in finding the front door of the building, but Neel hesitated before he opened it. Costa had been sure Neel could get away without being noticed, but he didn't feel so sure himself. There certainly would be plenty of police in the streets, even here. Only as he eased the door did he understand why Costa had been so positive about this.

Gunfire hammered somewhere behind him; other guns answered. Costa must have had another gun. He had planned it this way and the best thing Neel could do was not to think about it and go ahead with the plan. A car whined by in the roadway. As soon as it had passed Neel slipped out and crossed the empty street to the nearest monosub entrance. Most of the stations had valet machines.

It was less than an hour later when he reached Hengly's apartment. Washed, shaved—and with his clothes cleaned—Neel felt a little more sure of himself. No one had stopped him or even noticed him. The lobby had been empty and the automatic elevator left him off at the right floor when he gave it Hengly's name. Now, facing the featureless door, he had a sharp knife of fear. It was too easy. He reached out slowly and tried the handle. The door was unlocked. Taking a deep breath, he opened it and stepped inside.

It was a large room, but unlit. An open door at the other end had a dim light shining through it. Neel started that way and pain burst in his head, spinning him down, face forward.

He never quite lost consciousness, but details were vague in his memory. When full awareness returned he realized that the lights were on in the room. He was lying on his back, looking up at them. Two men stood next to him, staring down at him from above the perspective columns of their legs. One held a short metal bar that he kept slapping into his open palm.

The other man was Hengly.

"Not very friendly for an old classmate," he said, holding out Neel's gun. "Now get inside, I want to talk to you."

Neel rolled over painfully and crawled to his feet. His head throbbed with pain, but he tried to ignore it. As he stood up his hand brushed his ankle. The tiny gun Costa had given him was still in the top of his shoe. Perhaps Hengly wasn't being as smart as he should.

"I can take care of him," Hengly said to the man with the metal rod. "He's the only one left now, so you can get some sleep. See you early in the morning though." The man nodded agreement and left.

Slouched in the chair Neel looked forward to a certain pleasure in killing Hengly. Costa was dead, and this man was responsible for his death. It wouldn't even be like killing a friend, Hengly was very different from the man he had known. He had put on a lot of weight and affected a thick beard and flowing mustache. There was something jovial and paternal about him—until you looked into his eyes. Neel slumped forward, worn out, letting his fingers fall naturally next to the gun in his shoe. Hengly couldn't see his hand, the desk was in the way. All Neel had to do was draw and fire.

"You can pull out the gun," Hengly said with a grim smile, "but don't try to shoot it." He had his own gun now, aimed directly at Neel. Leaning forward he watched as Neel carefully pulled out the tiny weapon and threw it across the room. "That's better," he said, placing his own gun on the desk where he could reach it easily. "Now we can talk."

"There's nothing I have to say to you, Hengly." Neel leaned back in the chair, exhausted. "You're a traitor!"

Hengly hammered the desk in sudden anger and shouted. "Don't talk to me of treachery, my little man of peace. Creeping up with a gun to kill a friend. Is that peaceful? Where are the ethos of humanism now, you were very fond of them when we were in the University!"

Neel didn't want to listen to the words, he thought instead of how right Costa had been. He was dead, but this was still his operation. It was going according to plan.

"Walk right in there," Costa had said. "He won't kill you. Not at first, at least. He's the loneliest man in the universe, because he has given up one world for another that he hasn't gained yet. There will be no one he can confide in. He'll know you have come to kill him, but he won't be able to resist talking to you first. Particularly if you make it easy for him to defeat you. Not too easy—he must feel he is outthinking you. You'll have a gun for him to take away, but that will be too obvious. This small gun will be hidden as well, and when he finds that, too, he should be taken off his guard. Not much, but enough for you to kill him. Don't wait. Do it at the first opportunity."

*

Out of the corner of his eye, Neel could see the radiophone clipped to the front of his jacket. It was slightly tarnished, looking like any one of ten thousand in daily use—almost a duplicate of the one Hengly wore. A universal symbol of the age, like the keys and small change in his pockets.

Only Neel's phone was a deadly weapon. Product of a research into sudden death that he had never been aware of before. All he had to do was get it near Hengly, the mechanism had been armed when he put it on. It had a range of two feet. As soon as it was that far from any part of his body it would be actuated.

"Can I ask you a question, Hengly?" His words cut loudly through the run of the other man's speech.

Hengly frowned at the interruption, then nodded permission. "Go ahead," he said. "What would you like to know?"

"The obvious. Why did you do it? Change sides I mean. Give up a positive work, for this ... this negative corruption...."

"That's how much you know about it." Hengly was shouting now. "Positive, negative. War, peace. Those are just words, and it took me years to find it out. What could be more positive than making something of my life—and of this planet at the same time. It's in my power to do it, and I've done it."

"Power, perhaps that's the key word," Neel said, suddenly very tired. "We have the stars now but we have carried with us our little personal lusts and emotions. There's nothing wrong with that, I suppose, as long as we keep them personal. It's when we start inflicting them on others the trouble starts. Well, it's over now. At least this time."

With a single, easy motion he unclipped the radiophone and flipped it across the desk towards Hengly.

"Good-by," he said.

The tiny mechanism clattered onto the desk and Hengly leaped back, shouting hoarsely. He pulled the gun up and tried to aim at the radiophone and at Neel at the same time. It was too late to do either. There was a brief humming noise from the phone.

Neel jerked in his chair. It felt as if a slight electric shock had passed through him. He had felt only a microscopic percentage of the radiation.

Hengly got it all. The actuated field of the device had scanned his nervous system, measured and tested it precisely. Then adjusted itself to the exact micro-frequency that carried the messages in his efferent nervous system. Once the adjustment had been made, the charged condensers had released their full blasts of energy on that frequency.

The results were horribly dramatic. Every efferent neuron in his system carried the message full power. Every muscle in his body responded with a contraction of full intensity.

Neel closed his eyes, covered them, turned away gasping. It couldn't be watched. An epileptic in a seizure can break the bones in a leg or arm by simultaneous contraction of opposing muscles. When all the opposed muscles of Hengly's body did this the results were horrible beyond imagining.

*

When Neel recovered a measure of sanity he was in the street, running. He slowed to a walk, and looked around. It was just dawn and the streets were empty. Ahead was the glowing entrance of a monotube and he headed for it. The danger was over now, as long as he was careful.

Pausing on the top step, he breathed the fresh air of the new morning. There was a sighing below as an early train pulled into the station. The dawn-lit sky was the color of blood.

"Blood," he said aloud. Then, "Do we have to keep on killing? Isn't there another way?"

He started guiltily as his voice echoed in the empty street, but no one had heard him.

Quickly, two at a time, he ran down the steps.